The Story of Colors

La Historia de los Colores

by Subcomandante Marcos

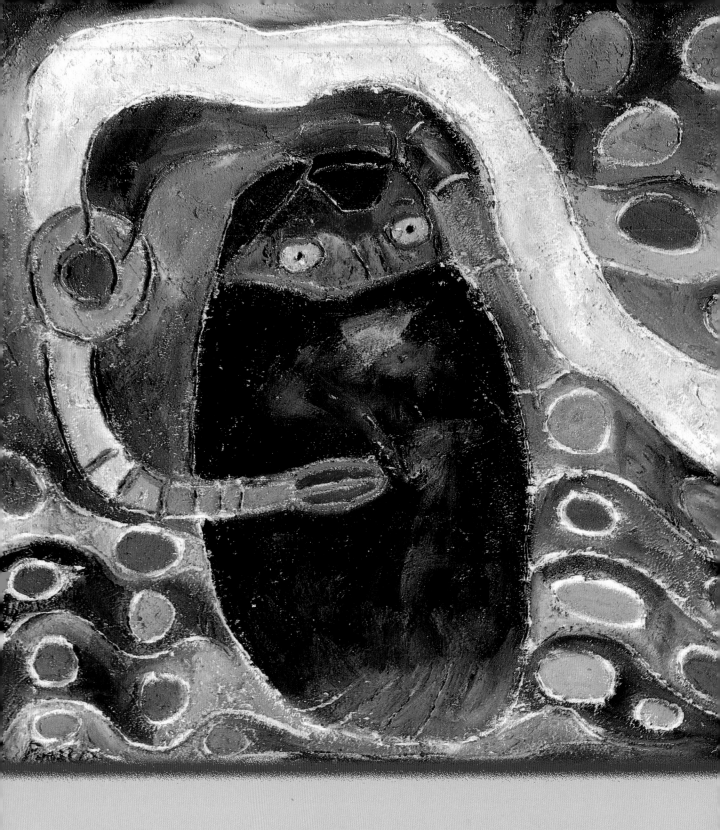

Enciendo la pipa y, después de las tres bocanadas de rigor, empiezo a contarles, tal y como la platicó el viejo *Antonio*...

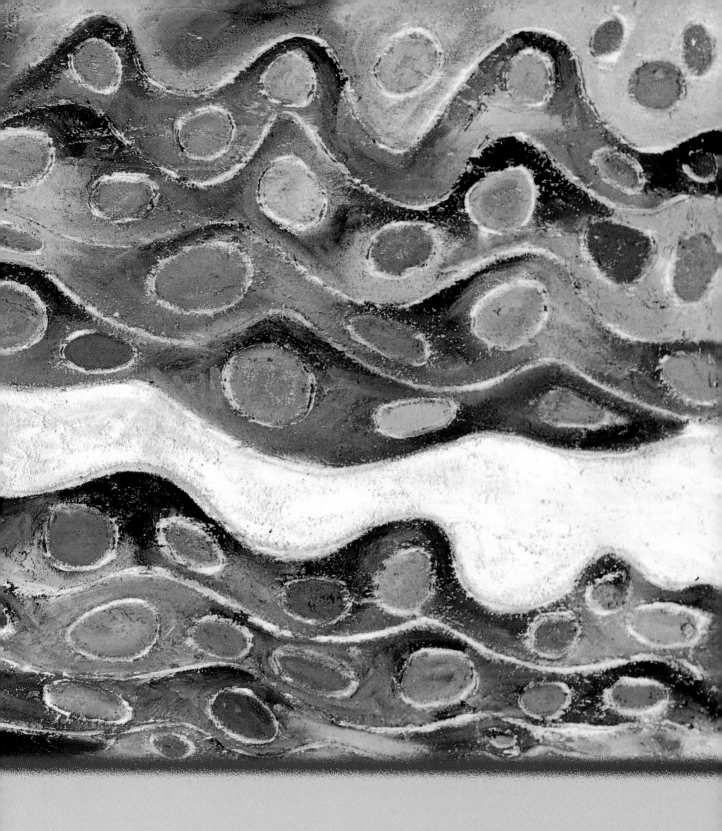

I light my pipe and, after three ceremonial puffs, I begin to tell you—just the way old Antonio used to tell it—

The Story of Colors

El viejo *Antonio* señala una guacamaya que cruza la tarde. "Mira", dice.
Yo miro ese hiriente rayo de colores en el marco gris de una lluvia
anunciándose. "Parecen mentira tantos colores para un solo pájaro", digo al
alcanzar la punta del cerro.

Old Antonio points at a macaw crossing in the afternoon sky. "Look," he says. I see the brilliant streak of colors in the gray mist of a gathering rain. "You wouldn't believe one bird could have so many colors," I say as I come to the top of the hill.

El viejo *Antonio* se sienta en una pequeña ladera libre del lodo que invade este camino real. Recobra la respiración mientras forja un nuevo cigarro. Yo me doy cuenta, apenas unos pasos adelante, que él quedó atrás.

Old Antonio sits down on a hillside where the mud isn't spilling onto the main road. He catches his breath while he rolls another cigarette. A few steps further on, I see that he's lingered behind.

Me vuelvo y me siento a su lado. "¿Usted cree que llegaremos al pueblo antes de que llueva?", le pregunto mientras enciendo la pipa. El viejo *Antonio* parece no escuchar. Ahora es una parvada de tucanes lo que distrae su vista. En su mano el cigarro espera el fuego para iniciar el lento dibujo del humo. Carraspea, da fuego al cigarro y se acomoda, como puede, para iniciar, lentamente.

I go back and sit down beside him. While I'm lighting my pipe, I ask him, "Do you think we'll get to the village before the rain starts?" Old Antonio doesn't seem to hear me. This time, it's a flock of toucans that's distracted him. The cigarette in his hand is waiting to be lit to start its lazy design of smoke. He clears his throat, lights the cigarette, makes himself as comfortable as he can and slowly begins his story.

"No así era la guacamaya. Acaso tenía colores. Puro gris era. Sus plumas eran rabonas, como gallina mojada. Una más entre tanto pájaro que a saber cómo se llegó al mundo porque los dioses no se sabían quién y cómo había hecho los pájaros.

"The macaw didn't used to be like this. It hardly had any color at all. It was just gray. Its feathers were stunted, like a wet chicken—just one more bird among all the others who didn't know how he arrived in the world. The gods themselves didn't know who made the birds. Or why.

Y así era de por sí. Los dioses despertaron después de que la noche había dicho "Hasta aquí nomás" al día. Y los hombres y mujeres se estaban dormidos o amándose, que es una forma bonita de cansarse para dormirse luego.

"And that's the way it was. The gods woke up after Night had said to Day, 'Okay, that's it for me—your turn.' And the men and women were sleeping or they were making love, which is a nice way to become tired and then go to sleep.

Los dioses peleaban, siempre peleaban estos dioses que salieron muy peleoneros, no como los primeros, los siete dioses que nacieron el mundo, los más primeros. Y los dioses peleaban porque muy aburrido estaba el mundo con sólo dos colores que lo pintaban.

Y era cierto el enojo de los dioses porque sólo dos colores se turnaban al mundo: el uno era el negro que mandaba la noche, el otro era el blanco que caminaba el día, y el tercero no era color, era el gris que pintaba tardes y madrugadas para que no brincaran tan duro el negro y el blanco.

"The gods were fighting. They were always fighting. They were very quarrelsome, these gods, not like the first ones, the seven gods who gave birth to the world, the very first ones. And the gods were fighting because the world was very boring with only two colors to paint it.

"And the anger of the gods was a true anger because only the two colors took their turns with the world: the black which ruled the night and the white which strolled about during the day. And there was a third which wasn't a real color. It was the gray which painted the dusks and the dawns so that the black and the white didn't bump into each other so hard.

Y eran estos dioses peleoneros pero sabedores. Y en una reunión que se hicieron sacaron el acuerdo de hacer los colores más largos para que fuera alegre el caminar y el amar de los hombres y mujeres murciélago.

Uno de los dioses agarró en caminar para pensar mejor su pensamiento y tanto pensaba su pensamiento que no miró su camino y se tropezó en una piedra así de grande y se pegó en su cabeza y le salió sangre de su cabeza.

"And these gods were quarrelsome but wise. They had a meeting and they finally agreed to make more colors. They wanted to make it more joyous for men and women—who were blind as bats—to take a walk or to make love.

"One of the gods took to walking so that he could think better. And he thought his thoughts so deeply that he didn't look where he was going. And he tripped on a stone so big that he hit his head and it started to bleed.

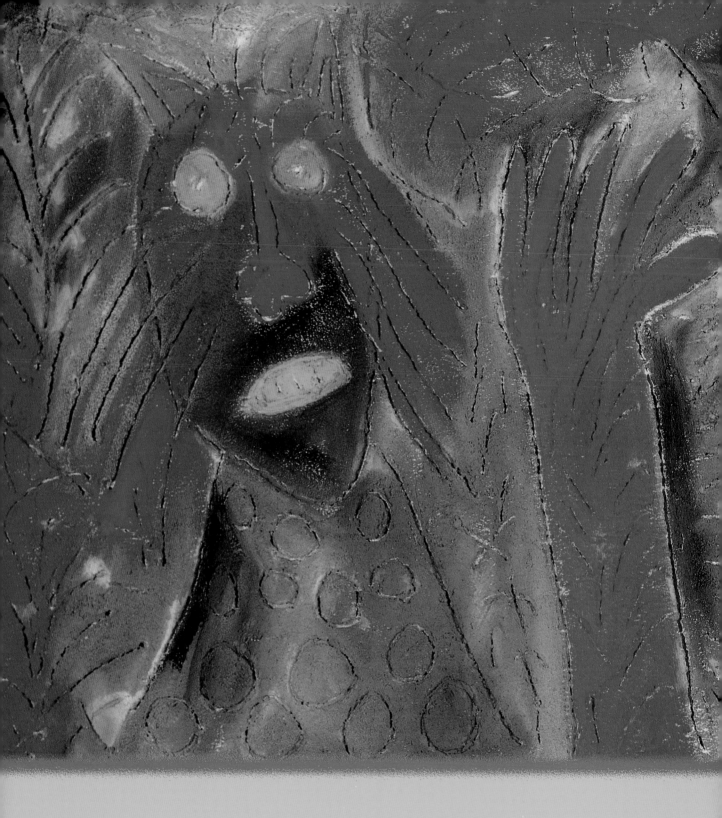

Y el dios, luego que pasó chilla y chilla un buen rato, la miró su sangre y la vio que es otro color que no es los dos colores. Y fue corriendo a donde estaban los demás dioses y les mostró el color nuevo y "colorado" le pusieron a ese color, el tercero que nacía.

"And the god, after screaming and squawking for quite a while, looked at his blood and saw that it was a different color, one that wasn't like the other two colors. And he went running to where the other gods were and showed them the new color, and they called this color *red*, the third color to be born.

Después, otro de los dioses buscaba un color para pintar la esperanza. Lo encontró después de un buen rato, fue y lo mostró en la asamblea de los dioses y "verde" le pusieron a ese color, el cuarto.

"Another god went straight upwards. 'I want to see what color the world is,' he said and kept climbing and climbing all the way up. When he got very high up, he looked down and saw the color of the world, but he didn't know how to bring it to where the other gods were so he kept looking for a long while until he became blind, because the color of the world stuck to his eyes. He came down as best he could, by fits and starts, and he arrived where the assembly of the gods was and said to them, 'I am carrying the color of the world in my eyes,' and they named the sixth color *blue.*

Otro dios estaba buscando colores cuando escuchó que un niño se reía, se acercó con cuidado y, cuando se descuidó el niño, el dios le arrebató la risa y lo dejó llorando. Por eso dicen que los niños de repente están riendo y de repente están llorando. El dios llevó la risa del niño y "amarillo" le pusieron a ese séptimo color.

"Another god was looking for colors when he heard a child laughing. He snuck up on the child quietly and, when the child wasn't paying attention, the god snatched his laugh and left him in tears. That's why they say that children can be laughing one minute and all of a sudden they are crying. The god stole the child's laugh and they called this seventh color *yellow*.

Para entonces los dioses ya estaban cansados y se fueron a tomar pozol y a dormirse y los dejaron a los colores en una cajita, botada bajo una ceiba. La cajita no estaba bien cerrada y los colores se salieron y empezaron a hacer alegría y se amaron y salieron más colores diferentes y nuevos y la ceiba lo miró todo y los tapó para que la lluvia no los borrara a los colores y cuando llegaron los dioses ya no eran siete colores sino bastantes y la miraron a la ceiba y le dijeron: "Tú pariste los colores, tú cuidarás el mundo y desde tu cabeza pintaremos el mundo".

"By now the gods were tired and they drank some pozol and went to sleep, leaving the colors in a little box which they threw beneath the ceiba tree. The little box wasn't closed very tight and the colors escaped and started to play happily and to make love to one another, and more and different colors were made, new ones. The ceiba tree looked at them and covered them all to keep the rain from washing the colors away, and when the gods came back, there weren't just seven colors but many more. They looked at the ceiba tree and said, 'You gave birth to the colors. You will take care of the world. And from the top of your head we shall paint the world.'

Y se subieron al copete de la ceiba y desde ahí empezaron a aventar los colores así nomás y el azul se quedó parte en el agua y parte en el cielo, y el verde le cayó a los árboles y las plantas, y el café, que era más pesado, se cayó en la tierra, y el amarillo, que era una risa de niño, voló hasta pintar el sol, el rojo llegó en su boca de los hombres y de los animales y lo comieron y se pintaron de rojo por dentro, y el blanco y el negro ya de por sí estaban en el mundo, y era un relajo cómo aventaban los colores los dioses, ni se fijaban dónde llega el color que avientan y algunos colores salpicaron a los hombres y por eso hay hombres de distintos colores y de distintos pensamientos.

"And they climbed to the top of the ceiba tree, and from there they started to fling colors all over the place, and the blue stayed partly in the sky and partly in the water, the green fell on the plants and the trees, and the brown, which was heavier, fell to the ground, and the yellow, which was a child's laugh, flew up to paint the sun. The red dropped into the mouths of men and animals and they ate it and painted themselves red inside. And the black and the white were, of course, already in the world. And it was a mess the way the gods threw the colors because they didn't care where the colors landed. Some colors splattered on the men and women, and that is why there are peoples of different colors and different ways of thinking.

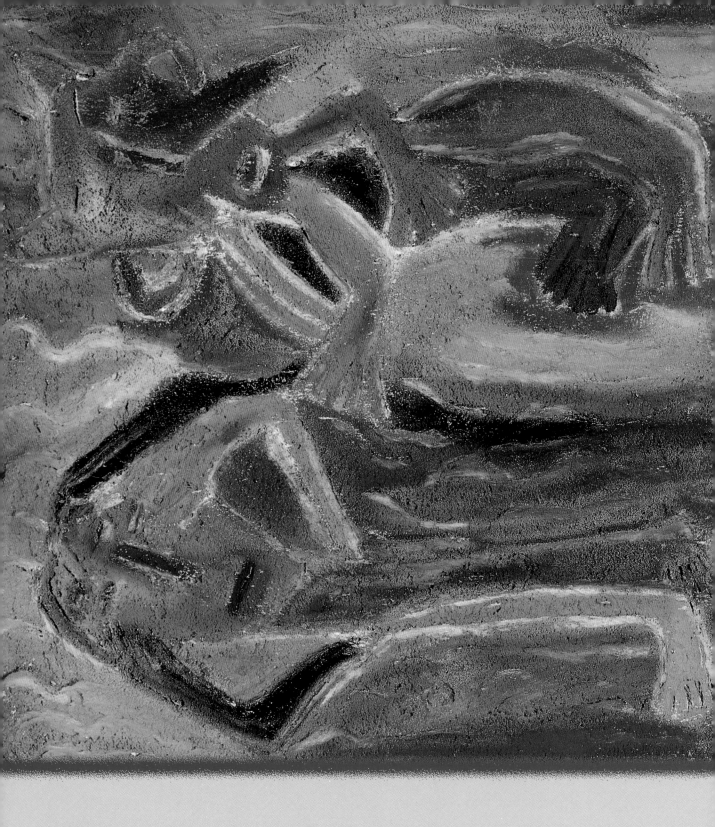

Y ya luego se cansaron los dioses y se fueron a dormir otra vez. Puro dormir querían estos dioses que no eran los primeros, los que nacieron el mundo. Y, entonces, para no olvidarse de los colores y no se fueran a perder, buscaron modo de guardarlos.

"And soon the gods got tired and went to sleep again. These gods just wanted to sleep. They weren't like the first ones, the ones who gave birth to the world. And then, because they didn't want to forget the colors or lose them, they looked for a way to keep them safe.

Y se estaba pensando en su corazón cómo hacer cuando la vieron a la guacamaya y entonces la agarraron y le empezaron a poner encima todos los colores y le alargaron las plumas para que cupieran todos. Y así fue como la guacamaya se agarró color y ahí lo anda paseando, por si a los hombres y mujeres se les olvida que muchos son los colores y los pensamientos, y que el mundo será alegre si todos los colores y todos los pensamientos tienen su lugar".

"And they were thinking about that in their hearts when they saw the macaw, and they grabbed it and started to pour all the colors on it and they stretched its feathers so that the colors could all fit. And that was how the macaw took hold of the colors, and so it goes strutting about just in case men and women forget how many colors there are and how many ways of thinking, and that the world will be happy if all the colors and ways of thinking have their place."

The End

Originally published in Mexico in 1996 as La Historia de los Colores by Ediciones Colectivo Callejero, Guadalajara.

The Story of Colors / La Historia de los Colores, A Folktale from the Jungles of Chiapas. For reasons of conscience and political circumstances, Subcomandante Marcos refuses all privileges of copyright for the text of this story, and, therefore, any person may use the text for his or her own use. Translation copyright © 1999 by Cinco Puntos Press. Illustrations copyright © 1996 by Colectivo Callejero. Photograph of Subcomandante Insurgente Marcos © by Corbis-Bettman. Printed in Hong Kong by Morris Press Limited. All rights reserved. No part of this book may be used or reproduced in any manner whatsoever without written consent from the publisher, except for brief quotations for reviews. For further information, write Cinco Puntos Press, 701 Texas Avenue, El Paso, TX 79901; or call 1-915-838-1625, or log on to our web site (www.cincopuntos.com).

FIRST EDITION
10 9 8 7 6 5 4 3 2 1

Library of Congress Cataloging-in-Publication Data

Marcos, subcomandante.
    [Historia de los colores, English & Spanish]
    The story of colors = La historia de los colores ; a
folktale from the jungles of Chiapas / by Subcomandante Marcos ;
with illustrations by Domitila Dominguez ; translated by Anne Bar
Din.
    p.cm.
    ISBN 0-938317-71-7 (paperback)
1. Mayas—Folklore. 2. Colors—Folklore. 3.
Tales—Mexico—Chiapas. I. Title.
    F1435.3.F6 M3713 1999
    398.2'0972'7507—dc21
                         98-43452
                         CIP

This book is published with the generous support of the Lannan Foundation. They stepped in when we needed it. ¡Muchísimas gracias!

The text for La Historia de los Colores is taken from the communiqué dated October 27, 1994 from Subcomandante Insurgente Marcos to the Mexican People.

A Note on the Translation: To many, Marcos' language, syntactical structures and punctuation may seem idiosyncratic. It's been noted in several places that his conversational writing is influenced by the Spanish of the indigenous people around him, and their Spanish is, of course, their second language. This makes for difficulties in the translation. We have tried to keep as close to the original as possible, but also we wanted to make the story a comfortable book to read. It is, after all, a storytelling.

Many thanks to the people who gave us their help in publishing this book: Steve Stacey, Suzan Kern, John Byrd, Joe Hayes, Suzy Morris, Antonio Ramírez Chavez, Anne Bar Din, Luis Mario Cerda and all the good people of the Colectivo Callejero.

Cover design and book design by Geronimo Garcia of El Paso, Texas